This book belongs to:

. . . .

SLIME?

It's Not Mine!

CLARE HELEN WELSH   NICOLA O'BYRNE

MACMILLAN CHILDREN'S BOOKS

Lenny the lemur was on holiday in sunny California. He was having lots of fun in the towering redwood trees.

But swinging from branch to branch was hungry work. He was about to break for a tasty bite to eat when . . .

. . . Lenny's fur was covered in a **sticky, icky** goo!
"I've been slimed!" he said, wiping the ooze with a leaf.

"**Slime? It's not mine,**" yawned a salamander from a nearby tree trunk. "Although my skin is covered in the stuff. It's how I breathe."

"Wow," said Lenny, taking a closer look. "But if it wasn't you, then who? **Who made all this goo?**"

"Slime? It's not mine!"
said the opossum snoozing in a hollow.

"My slime is **smelly** and comes from my bottom.
It stops other animals eating me."

"Too much information!" said Lenny, backing away.
He didn't need all the details. He just needed to find the
sticky slime-maker and get back to his snack.

"It must have been
someone," he said.
"Who else makes goo?"

"Maybe it was slime mould," offered the opossum. "It's all over the woods."

"Are you the slime that committed the crime?" said Lenny, wagging his finger at a blob of yellow slime.

"It can't hear you and it can't reply," the opossum pointed out. "Slime mould isn't an animal. It isn't even a plant . . ."

But it didn't matter. The slime mould wasn't nearly **gooey** or **gunky** enough.

"I'll find that **icky, sticky** slime-maker, if it's the last thing I do!" said Lenny. "Then I'll have my tasty bite to eat."

Lenny climbed down the cliffs and onto the beach.

"Slime? It's not mine . . . is it?" said a Sheephead fish grazing on the rocks. "I burp slimy sleeping balloons to protect me from predators. Want to see?"

Lenny could hardly
believe his ears . . .

. . . or his eyes! But up close it was clear that the fish's
slimy balloon wasn't the goo he was looking for either.

"My mistake," said the fish. "Your slime sounds much sloppier."

"Sloppy slime? Is it mine?" asked a dolphin playing close to the shore. "I spray water and slime from my blowhole. Almost all sea creatures use slime in one way or another."

The dolphin's fountain was impressive, but it wasn't at all like the **icky, sticky** slime that Lenny was covered in.

Poor Lenny was no closer
to solving the crime.
He was **gooey** and **gunky**
and hungrier than ever.

"I think I'll have my tasty bite to eat,"
he said. "It might help me think."
But as he turned to leave . . .

"Sorry, it's mine!" called a sea lion
lounging on the rocks. "I use slime to keep my
eyes and nose moist. I can spit it long distances, too."
The sea lion's slime was definitely **oozy** and **gloopy**, but . . .

. . . it still wasn't the **sticky, icky** goo that Lenny was looking for. "Lemurs make slime too," he huffed. "But we don't feel the need to spray it, wipe it, burp it, fling it, spit it or leave it lying all over the place!"

"Really?" said the animals. "You make slime as well?"

"Sure, in my nose. It helps me get rid of germs."

"You don't pick out your slime with your fingers, do you?" said the sea lion. "I've seen humans do that. Terrible manners."

"No way!" said Lenny. "I wouldn't **EVER** use my fingers. I clean my nose . . ."

"... with my tongue!"

SHHHLLLLP!

And to show the animals
exactly what he meant . . .
Lenny licked both his
nostrils clean, except a
little bit for later.

No one said anything. Nothing at all. Although the sea lion was very impressed. "Bravo!" he clapped.

"It's snot a big deal," said Lenny proudly.

Lenny sat down in a nice quiet spot on the edge of the beach and picked out a tasty bite to eat. He was sure he was never going to solve his **icky, sticky** slime crime when . . .

"HELP!"

. . . . he heard something faint and far, far away.

"The slime is mine!" Or maybe it was someone very small.

Lenny looked around. But there was no one.

"Down here!" called a voice from underneath Lenny, and a little slug slithered into view.

"Slugs use slime to slide along the ground. Mine is like glue. If I think I'm in danger, I slime myself to my surroundings. I've been stuck to you the whole time – sorry!"

But there was no need to apologise.
Lenny was delighted. The **icky, sticky**
slime crime had been solved!

Carefully Lenny carried the slug back into the woods. Then, he picked a nice, clean, slime-free place to have his snack.

"YUMMY!"

Finally, it was time to eat the tasty treat he'd waited such a long time for. But just as he was about to tuck in, Lenny stopped.

All the **icky, sticky** slime talk had put him right off his fruit!

"Never mind," said Lenny, putting his snack to one side. "I know something that'll hit the spot perfectly . . ."

FACTS AND SNAPS!

Arboreal Salamanders breathe through their skin, which is covered in slime to keep it nice and damp.

Whatever you do, don't scare an **Opossum**! If threatened, opossums pretend to be dead and release a smelly, green slime from their bottom.

Slime Mould isn't a plant or an animal . . . but a mass of simple cells, which can move and even solve mazes. Wow!

At night, the **California Sheephead Fish** burps out a slimy sleeping sack and wraps itself up. The slime stops predators from sniffing them out. Cosy!

Like humans, **Lemurs** produce slime in their nose. Lemurs lick their noses to keep them clean. What do you do?!

Dolphins blast a mixture of air, water and slime through their blowholes. It's called 'chuffing'.

Never get too close to a **Sea Lion**. They're known for their slimy, long-distance spits and sneezes.

The **Dusky Arion Slug** produces a slime so sticky that scientists are using it to create new medical super-glues.

For the Kellands – C.H.W.
For Laura, Will, Ly, Erica, Irvin, and all the
other healthcare professionals – N.O'B.

First published 2022 by Macmillan Children's Books
an imprint of Pan Macmillan
The Smithson, 6 Briset Street, London, EC1M 5NR
EU representative: Macmillan Publishers Ireland Ltd, 1st Floor,
The Liffey Trust Centre, 117–126 Sheriff Street Upper,
Dublin 1, D01 YC43
Associated companies throughout the world
www.panmacmillan.com

ISBN: 978-1-5290-6445-2 (PB)
ISBN: 978-1-5290-8338-5 (EB)

9 8 7 6 5 4 3 2 1

A CIP catalogue record for this book is available from the British Library.

Printed in China.